Plant People

More **Strange Matter**™ from
Marty M. Engle & Johnny Ray Barnes, Jr.

Plant People

Johnny Ray Barnes, Jr.

**A
MONTAGE
PUBLICATION**

Montage Publications, a Front Line company,
San Diego, California

ISBN 1-56714-053-X

Printed in the U.S.A.

TO KAREN
(THE ORIGINAL BAD SEED)

1

I'm killing it, I thought.

My teeth ground the living thing practically in two, before it had a chance to get stubborn.

Its flavorless, wet core—*its backbone*—became a stringy mess. I'd have to tug it apart.

I held it tightly in my jaws and pulled with my fist.

SNAP. It separated.

Chomping away, I could only think about one thing; spines. Celery is a vegetable, but it has a spine. I'd read that somewhere, and not in the *National Exclaimer*, either, like my mom claimed. I knew it for a fact. Crunching down on the last bits of it in my mouth, I asked myself — *if a vegetable has a spine, could it possibly be alive?*

If so, *I'd just killed it.*

"Bye-bye, appetite," I groaned, and tossed what remained of the stalk to the ground.

I never liked most vegetables anyway. Or even meat, for that matter. I'm Rachel Pearson, microwavarian. Canned pasta, boxed fish sticks, nachos with cheese; anything I can heat and eat in five minutes or less.

That *was* my diet. But then I decided to try out for cheerleading. My mother's been stuffing gardens down my throat ever since. *To make the cheerleading squad, you'll have to be in top shape,* Mom says.

I'd almost made it through my Saturday afternoon without any vegetables, but then Mom called me to the door and dropped a handful of celery in my hand. I didn't grumble, though. I just took them, knowing I'd ditch them in the woods . . . *on the way to the new house.*

By "new house," I mean the one being built just up the hill from ours, beyond a small patch of woods that separates the two lots. It's the first new house to be built in my neighborhood in three years. This weekend, while the workers aren't there, will be my best chance to explore it. Mom and Dad warned me not to be nosy and to stay away from it, but they just don't

2

understand. It's in my blood.

When it comes right down to it, I'm not really nosy. Just overly curious. I like to know what's going on in very boring places. Who cares what's going on with the cutest couple in school, or what the class clown did to be sent to the principal's office this time? These are obvious, popular concerns.

I like to dig a little deeper. Like that kid in the back of class who reads a lot and never talks to anyone; *what's he all about?* Or the teacher that disappears from class for the same ten minutes every day. *What's up with that?* Or a house that's in the middle of being built. *What's it going to look like? Are there any secret rooms?* These are the questions that drive me crazy.

Clearing the brush, I approached the wooden skeleton that would someday be a home. The bright sunlight gave it an almost grandiose feeling.

It's almost a shame to finish it, I thought. *It's cool the way it is.*

A single, wide board served as my only bridge to the house. It crossed over a huge trench that circled the foundation. At the bottom of the trench, mud galore. I crossed the board quickly, feeling it creak only once toward the middle. But I made it across, and once inside, gazed around excitedly.

I'm tiny, standing in a house made of matches, I imagined. Everywhere I looked there was wood, either nailed on its side or standing vertically. Sawdust covered the floors, and empty cola cans and candy wrappers littered the rooms.

"What a fortress of solitude this would make," I said aloud, already hoping funding would run out for construction and they'd have to leave the house the way it stood.

Then I saw the stairs.

The next level. I had to get there.

Dirty footprints stained each step, forcing me to double-check my nerve. *Construction workers don't work on Saturdays do they? Would I get in trouble for trespassing?*

Before I could talk myself out of going any farther, my feet trotted up the stairs to the next floor.

"Hallelujah," I sighed at the top. No one there, leaving me free to roam in peace.

The entire floor had a warm, yellow glow from the sunlight, and I could look up through the rafters at Fairfield's blue sky.

4

Through the window frame, there would be an almost perfect view of the neighborhood, obscured only by the small wooded area I had crossed to get there.

I'd be able to see everything if I could get up a little higher . . .

Now if my mom could have seen me at that moment, she would have had a fit. She would say . . . *You shouldn't be at the site. You shouldn't be in the house. You shouldn't climb into those rafters . . .*

The imagined scoldings faded in my mind as I scaled the wall frame to its top board. Reaching carefully for the A-shaped supports, I stood up through what would soon be a roof, and took in the view.

Awesome. Total freedom. Just as I suspected, I could see the entire neighborhood. As the birds sang the songs of the day, I took in all of the activity. Sheriff Drake's son Russell mowing their lawn. The entire Reece family piling into their car for a day at the YMCA swimming pool. Waylon Burst peeking out of his window across the street from my house . . .

Mom stepping out the back door and calling my name!

"RACHEL!"

My mind screamed for me to duck.

She didn't see me, but she wouldn't stop searching. She wouldn't stop calling my name.

Which meant I had to get down and out of there. Fast.

Just as I lowered my feet to the closest board, *I saw something strange.*

In the woods behind my house.

Slightly to the right of the path I took to the construction site.

Something moved.

Something . . . unusual.

It stopped me from moving another inch.

It made me forget about Mom.

In fact, I couldn't even hear the birds singing anymore.

Focusing my attention on the spot, I waited. My joints started hurting from the awkward position, but I wouldn't budge.

You see, things don't move like I had just seen this thing move. There seemed to be too much of it, flowing in and out of the brush.

Curling.

Sneaking.

And there it was again!

6

This time I saw it clearly. Long, light-colored tentacles, moving like snakes, but through the air. Large, white spaghetti, spreading out over the entire wooded area until . . .

"RACHEL!"

Mom called out to me again, and the thing stopped moving. Then it pulled its way back into the bushes. When Mom yelled for the final time . . .

"RACHEL! TESSA'S ON THE PHONE FOR YOU!"

. . . the thing slipped away. It pulled itself through the wooded patch as if it were yanked, and in the ensuing moments everything grew still again.

But the birds stayed quiet.

Mom kept calling my name.

And to my horror, I could see something else down there.

Something moving. Something . . . big.

And to get back to my house, *I'd have to walk right past it.*

I didn't want to tear my eyes away. From my position, I could see where it was. If I jumped down and ran to the bottom floor, I'd lose track of it. The thing could be waiting for me as soon as I stepped across the plank bridge.

That's why I kept eyeing the large dirt pile next to the house. The mound stood very high, almost as tall as the roof. Definitely within jumping distance.

Inching my way across the boards, the mountain of earth soon came within pouncing distance. Every muscle in my body tensed, ready to push away from the roof.

Was I being just a little too paranoid?

No. As soon as you start thinking that, they'll get you. It's always best to go by instinct.

So I jumped.

My feet hit first. Then my knees, my hands, and right after that, my face smashed right down into the dirt. I saw stars while I rolled to the bottom of the hill. I ended up flat on my back with my mouth full of gritty-tasting dirt.

My face was wet.

Sitting up, I wiped the moisture from under my nose and my cheeks.

Blood.

I'd given myself a bloody nose on that stupid hill. With the very next breath I took, pain shot up my nasal passages, forcing me into motion.

I pressed the side of my hand under my nose to stop the bleeding, but the gusher wouldn't let up. Soon my entire hand was coated a sticky red. My eyes watered, leaving my head a thumping mess.

You're going to pass out, Rachel, I thought. *This thing's going to get you.*

Then the impossible happened.

In spite of the river coming out of my nostrils, *I smelled something.* Not the sweet, coppery smell of blood that had caked the lining of my nose, but something else.

Something nice.

So I stopped. I breathed in the scent again.

Mmmm . . . definitely a scent. Too nice to be called an odor. Too natural to be a perfume. But most certainly light-years beyond *a smell.*

Suddenly my body felt warm. My nose stopped bleeding. My head ceased to throb. And my feet started moving in the direction I had wanted to stay away from just seconds earlier.

My eyelids drooped halfway as I moved through the trees, searching for the source of the enticing aroma. I didn't seem to have any control.

Deer in the headlights. That's what kept running through my head. *The thing in the woods gives off a scent that completely hypnotizes its victim.* It wants me to come to it. I'm walking right into a death trap.

And with a few more steps, I stood right in front of it.

A large, green-and-yellow pumpkin, the size of a bean bag chair, completely split open with what looked like veiny guacamole leaking out of every crack. Beside it were three more, in exactly the same condition.

Normally, I automatically laugh at the unbelievable. But this time, I had no reaction at all. A buzzing in my head kept me from getting overly excited. And with my brain turning to pudding, I defaulted to just staring at the scene.

I watched the thick ooze drip from the shell, bubbling every now and again.

I suddenly had the strangest feeling that I was watching something die.

"RACHEL! WHERE ARE YOU?" Mom yelled.

My trance was broken.

Confusion came first. Then disgust.

But finally, my curiosity won out.

Even though it brought me closer to such a sickening sight than I ever thought I wanted to be, I reached down and grabbed a piece of the broken shell.

Then I turned around and ran, and never looked back.

TWO MONTHS LATER

"RACHEL! TESSA'S ON THE PHONE!"
Mom yelled up to my room.

"I'VE GOT IT!" I shouted back, dropping my *Discover* magazine to the floor, and bouncing for the telephone.

"Hey, what's up?" I asked, pulling the phone cord free from the junk on my floor.

"Nothing much. Just calling to see what went on this week," Tessa said.

Tessa Lewis is my best friend. I can't think of anyone else I'd rather talk with. We're a perfect match. There's only one thing that separates us. Two hundred miles.

"Nothing. What's happening in Mullinfield?" I asked back. Tessa's dad moved them to

12

Mullinfield a year and a half ago. We still check in with each other every weekend. This Saturday was her turn to call me.

"Come on, Rachel. Cheerleader tryouts were yesterday. What happened? How did you do?" she asked, sounding like a news reporter.

"No comment," I answered.

"COME ON! TELL ME!" she exploded.

"Tessa, I don't —"

"TELL ME."

"Okay. Nothing, all right? Nothing happened," I confessed.

Her voice suddenly grew softer.

"What do you mean nothing happened?" she asked.

"I mean nothing happened. I walked out in front of the entire student body, did my routine, and nothing happened. They didn't clap, they didn't jeer. They didn't have any reaction at all," I said, feeling a lump emerge in my throat halfway through the recollection.

"There had to have been *some* response," Tessa urged.

"Someone coughed," I admitted.

"I don't understand. Did you do the same routine you sent me on the videotape?" she asked.

13

"Yep."

"How could they just sit there after that?" she growled, growing more and more agitated.

"Because no one likes me, Tessa. Wait. Strike that. No one knows me enough to like me or not like me. I'm like the invisible kid around that school. I've told you that. Ever since you left I haven't had anyone to talk to."

"Rachel, stop sounding so pathetic. Did you make cheerleader or not?" Tessa never liked it when I whined to her.

"Tryouts got started late. No one had time to vote. I'll probably know by Monday afternoon," I sighed, regretting the experience and dreading the outcome all in one breath.

"Well, what are you doing now?" she asked.

"Reading. I went to the library and checked out some books and copied some magazine articles," I told her, picking up the science magazine from the floor.

"*YOU'RE STILL READING ABOUT PLANTS?*" she asked.

"Well, yeah. But you know what?" I asked back.

"You still haven't found your plant . . ."

"*I still haven't found my plant,*" I said,

flipping the pages back and forth. "I've been close a couple of times, but nothing matches the size, the color, or even the region. It could be a whole new variety for all I know!" I tossed the magazine onto the bed, then walked to my bookshelf.

"Have you told anyone about it?" Tessa seemed a little more interested.

"Yeah," I said. "I told Mom and Dad. Mom worried that it might be poisonous, and pretty much ordered me to stay away from it. But Dad went up and had a look."

"And?" she asked.

I removed two books from the shelf, revealing a tiny jar. Through the slight condensation clouding the inside, I could see the small piece of plant shell. It was still as vibrantly green now as it had been two months before, when I grabbed it.

"He didn't find anything," I said, picking up the jar and studying the sample. "There was nothing there."

"Do you think someone took them? I mean, even if they had completely died, there would have been something there," Tessa reasoned.

"I don't know what happened to the thing, *or things*. There was so much ooze lying every-where, I can't be sure it came from just one shell," I said. "Anyway, Dad says he believes me, but he really hasn't pursued it. Not like me."

I needed more light to get a better look in the jar. Moving to my window, I opened the shades and held the jar up to the brightness.

"Rachel," Tessa's voice grew soft, even lower than before. "Do you still have that piece of it?"

"Yeah," I answered, peering through the glass to study the plant's deep-jade color. For the first time I noticed the minuscule hairs that protruded from its skin, and its underside had collected little masses of gel that dripped to the bottom of the jar like a thick molasses. The shell itself looked porous, beading sweat almost like a human . . .

Then it moved.

"AAAAAAGGGGGHHH!" I screamed, dropping the jar and the phone to the floor.

My heart wanted to bounce out of my chest, so I breathed in and out deeply to slow it down. Tessa's scared voice shouted through the receiver but I didn't pick it up. I stared at the jar, waiting for its contents to spring to life again.

Only then did I notice something moving outside my window.

4

In the house behind mine—the one up on the hill that I'd explored two months earlier, *just before I saw those awful plants . . .*

Someone was moving in.

The house had only been finished for a couple of days, and people were already moving their things into it.

I must have seen them through the jar, I told myself. *That's what made the plant look like it had moved.*

It made sense. I made it make sense.

The people were unloading their belongings from a minivan, which usually meant there were kids. Sure enough, a man—a tall, plainly dressed man who had to be the father—handed one of the boxes to a boy who looked about my age. Then a woman wearing a light-colored sundress emerged from the van with a lamp, and gave it to a girl who also looked my age. Suddenly, they all stopped in unison, and turned to watch a moving truck pull up into the driveway and park. It cut off my view of the minivan entirely.

That's when I heard Tessa calling my name over the phone. Snapping to my senses, I picked up the receiver.

"Sorry," I said.

"What happened? Why did you scream?" she asked. I must have scared her out of her wits.

"I thought I saw—well, it was nothing. But hey, I've got new neighbors!" I actually felt a little excitement building in my voice.

"Any kids?" Tessa inquired, knowing that the only kids in my neighborhood were boys. There had never been a girl around for me to hang out with.

"Yeah. A boy and girl. He'll probably get sucked into the ranks of the Forest Oaks Boy Brigade. If she's smart, she won't try to follow." I'd once tried to join Waylon Burst and Shane Reece on one of their war adventures through the neighboring woods. They made me play the enemy, which meant they tossed mudballs at me all day.

"Why don't you go over there and meet them?" Tessa urged. She saw this as a great way for me to make some new friends and I knew it. Pretty noble of her.

"You know, I just might," I said.

Then someone knocked on my door.

"Yes?" I called.

Mom opened the door.

"Are you all right in here? I thought I heard you scream," she said with a concerned look on her face.

"I'm cool, Mom," I answered. "Tessa and I were just seeing who could scream the loudest."

My mom just shook her head.

"Two hundred miles apart and you two are still cutting up together. Well, listen, tell Tessa you'll call her later. Someone downstairs wants to meet you."

"Who?" I asked.

"The two children who just moved in behind us. They walked over and introduced themselves to me while I was out planting my azaleas. I told them about you and they wanted to meet you. So, come on down," she said.

"*Mom!* Why'd you have to do that?" I couldn't believe the way she fed me to the lions sometimes.

"Will you just come down? It'll do you good to get out of this dark room of yours," she said.

All was lost.

"Tessa, I'll call you back later," I told her.

"No problem." —*Get out of that dark room of yours*— "And tell your new neighbors I said 'Hi!'" she said.

"Sure thing." I hung up the phone as slowly as possible.

It's not that I didn't want to meet the new kids. I just wanted to be the first to say hello. I wanted to be the initiator. Now they'd beaten me to the punch and caught me off guard and ill prepared.

Trudging down the stairs, I saw two small bodies standing by the door. A boy and a girl. The boy wore simple jeans and the girl had on a sundress, almost like a smaller version of her mother's. As they came into full view, both of their heads snapped up, watching me with wide-eyed anticipation as I came down the stairs. And what eyes they had! I could swear their pupils grew larger with every step I took, making their eyes appear almost black.

A chill ran through my body as I hit the last step. It had suddenly gotten very cold.

"Rachel," Mom said. "This is Richard and Jane Smith. They're moving into the house on the hill today, and they wanted to get to know their closest neighbor."

"Hi," I said quickly. I wanted the first words to be mine.

"Hello, Rachel," Richard said. His voice sounded very clear and extremely direct.

"Hello, Rachel," echoed Jane, her speech as formal as her brother's.

I took it as my turn to reply, but my mind went blank. What followed was an unpleasant, awkward silence.

Mom rushed in to help.

"Richard and Jane say that their parents have given them a little break from moving. They'd like to take a look around the neighborhood, and I told them you'd be the perfect tour guide," she said.

Mom!

"Well, I would, but I can't go out looking like this . . ." I started to say.

"You look fine," interrupted Richard.

"It's just a walk," added Jane. "Besides, it's Saturday."

I couldn't argue with that logic. And they had obviously won Mom over pretty quickly. So I figured—why not?

"Let me go throw on some shoes," I said.

I walked up the stairs, pulled on my cross-trainers, and trudged back down to the foyer.

Richard and Jane waited for me in my front yard. When I saw them, that creepy feeling returned.

They just stood there in the middle of my yard, staring at me. They didn't talk to each other. They didn't even look around the neighborhood. Their eyes stayed fixed on me as I walked up to them, and I waited for them to say or *do* something.

"So," I finally started, "what do you guys want to see first? There's a creek at the end of the street, and a small park right at the entrance gate."

"Have you ever explored the hills around the neighborhood?" asked Richard.

I hadn't expected *that* question.

"Oh, yeah. I've been all through them. It's

one of my most favorite things to do," I said.

"We'd like to explore the hills," Jane said.

"Explore the hills? You're wearing a skirt. It'll probably get dirty," I replied.

"I'll be fine. Let's go," she said.

"Well . . ." I wanted to talk them out of it.

"I'd like to go to the one with all the trees on top," Richard cut in as he pointed over my shoulder. He seemed to like interrupting people when they were talking.

"That one?" I looked to the hill where he was pointing. It happened to be the same hill Waylon and Shane had chased me around. I hadn't been up there since.

"It will be fun, Rachel," Jane said.

I gave a heavy sigh.

"Just to let you guys know, my mom doesn't really like me wandering around these hills. If she finds out I've been up there, I'm in for nothing but trouble," I told them.

"We won't tell," said Richard. "We're friends."

Friends, already? Hardly, I thought. *But who knows? Maybe they've got the same bug I do. Maybe they just wanted to explore for exploring's sake. I'm just being too uptight.*

"Okay, let's go," I said.

I tried not to read too much into the conversation the Smith kids and I had on the way up to the hill. The two of them definitely asked a lot of questions, though. I suppose I should have expected a lot of curiosity from kids who'd just moved to a new neighborhood, but they asked some pretty bizarre things.

"Is rainfall a very common thing in Fairfield?" Richard asked as we reached the base of the hill.

Like I said, odd questions. We started up the incline as I struggled for an appropriate response.

"It rains," I answered, feeling a spark of sarcasm coming on. "I've even seen it."

I turned to give him a friendly smile, but

Jane blocked my view, and continued with the question.

"What he meant was, when the rain falls, does it fall often?" she asked. "Once a week? Once every two weeks? Is it an *annual* event?"

It seemed that I wasn't the only one with a smart tongue.

Using each tree trunk as a climber's helper, I pushed and pulled my way up the hill. I showed off, moving quickly up the incline like a monkey on a mission. Turning around to check Jane and Richard's reactions, I almost lost my balance when I saw Richard's face directly behind me.

"Quite a climb," he said, moving easily up beside, then past me.

What shocked me even more was that Jane, in that dress of hers, *had already topped the hill.* She slipped past me before I could make it up there myself.

"Wow! You guys are fast," I exclaimed when I got to the top and found Richard with his hand in the dirt, digging away.

Maybe my bad memories of being chased and bombarded on that hill took over, but I instantly assumed that Richard was constructing a dirt clod with my name on it. Scooping up a handful of dirt for myself, I cocked my arm, ready to fire.

"What are you doing?" came Jane's voice from behind me.

I dropped the dirt clod to the ground.

"Uh, nothing. Nothing. Just checking out the dirt. Nice and rich." Possibly the lamest excuse I could have come up with.

"It's the healthiest in this area," she said, sounding completely convincing.

When I turned to Richard, I saw him emptying the last bit of dirt from his hand into his pocket.

"What are *you* doing?" I asked. These two got stranger by the second.

"I collect bugs. This dirt will be good for their tanks," he said, wiping the last bits from his hand.

"Why didn't you bring a bucket or something?" My mom would kill me if I came home with a pocket full of dirt.

"Everything's still packed up. But I'll be back later with one. This is good soil. Very good soil," he answered.

"Richard," called Jane, looking down at the ground in front of her. "A spring beetle."

Richard and I walked closer to get a look. A large, black bug crawled just beside Jane's feet. When it stopped to chew on a leaf, Jane picked it up.

"I've been seeing those everywhere," I said softly, watching its legs move just a few inches from Jane's face.

"Spring beetles come out in armies this time of the year. I already have one for my collection. They are extremely easy to catch," Richard explained.

"Too easy to catch," said Jane. "But that's not the best thing about them."

"What's the best thing?" I asked.

To my horror, Jane held the beetle up over her head, then dropped it in her mouth. It instantly tried to climb out, but her teeth clamped down on its head, making its juice shoot in the air. She cracked the bug's shell in her mouth, chewing viciously until it became pasty. Then with a loud gulp, she swallowed the beetle.

"They're crunchy," she said.

"AAAAGGGGGHHHHH! HOW COULD YOU DO THAT?! WHAT'S THE MATTER

WITH YOU!?"

Richard's hand grabbed my shoulder.

"Relax, Rachel. Spring beetles are edible. They're a delicacy."

"GET YOUR HAND OFF ME, YOU WEIRDO! YOU'RE SICK IN THE HEAD! YOU AND YOUR BUG-EATING SISTER! JUST LEAVE ME ALONE!" I lost it. I backed away from them, searching for some kind of emotion in their blank stares. But they simply stepped closer to one another, watching me make my exit.

When I got to the edge of the hilltop, I took a quick look down, and then took off.

But as I left the hill, I realized something that made me run home even faster.

When Richard grabbed me, *I smelled something*. A very familiar scent, exactly like the one I had smelled two months before.

"Mom, listen to me. There is no way I'm eating dinner with those two psychos!" I declared as Mom chopped tomatoes for her spaghetti sauce.

"Rachel, I want you to stop this, right now. I want to get to know these people. We don't have any neighbors we can really do things with. The Reeces seem to always be on one vacation after another, and Sheriff Drake is married to his job. And I don't even want to discuss the Burst family and that son of theirs. But the Smiths seem like very nice, very normal people."

"Mom, Jane Smith ate a bug!" I exclaimed.

"Rachel, we don't know them very well yet. Maybe they spent some time overseas. Bugs are a delicacy in some countries," she answered.

"*Bugs are not a delicacy.* You can find them anywhere, at anytime and eat one of them. But nobody does it because they're *bugs!*" I tried to reason with her, but I could tell Mom was about to shut me off and pull rank.

"We're not discussing this any further," she said, sliding the tomatoes off the cutting board and into the pot. "It's Sunday. We're going to have a nice dinner. You're going to be nice to Richard and Jane while we get to know their parents, Tom and Betty."

Tom and Betty? The whole family had names from 1950s television. *How plain could you get?*

Then I heard the car door slam outside.

Dad. He was home from playing golf.

I went to the front door to greet him and see if he needed any help with his clubs. In other words, I'd get on *his* good side so he'd be on *my* side about the Smith family.

The door opened, followed by a grumble.

"The worst game I've played in twenty-one years," he muttered. "I hate golf."

Uh-oh, he didn't have a good side today. But I was desperate, and before he could throw his clubs on the floor I said, "Dad, Mom's invited the Smiths over for dinner tonight!"

Dad dropped his golf clubs. "AW, NO, Patty," he started yelling to Mom in the kitchen. "NO. I

DON'T WANT COMPANY TONIGHT. I HAD A LOUSY GAME. I'M TIRED. I want to watch *PIERWATCH . . .*"

"What you'll be watching is my happy face from your side of the table as we dine with the Smiths," Mom said, poking her head out of the kitchen with her mixing spoon in hand. "I've already had this discussion with Rachel and I'm not having it with you."

Dad groaned and looked down at me. "What are they like?" he asked.

"Weird," I said.

He groaned again and made his way upstairs.

Then the doorbell rang.

Mom shot out from the kitchen.

"That must be them," she said whispering. "Go ahead and get the door!"

I sighed and went to the door. When I opened it, Mr. Smith stepped right on in.

"Hello, Rachel. I'm Mr. Smith," he said. He spoke in the same commanding tone as his children, only deeper, and a little more chilling.

When I saw him from my window the day before, it hadn't registered how tall he was. But there, standing in the doorway, he had to be the most imposing man I'd ever met. Looking up at him, I felt as small as the spring beetle Jane had crunched the day before.

I realized I'd been silent for too long. "H-Hi. Come in."

That sounded stupid. He had already come in. Instead, he moved to the side, letting the rest of his family come through. First came Mrs. Smith, and then the two little freaks.

"I believe you've already met Richard and Jane. This is my wife, Betty," he said as she came forward and put a hand on each side of my face.

"Hello, Rachel," she said.

Then Mom made her entrance from the kitchen.

"I'm so glad you could make it," she said with the voice and attitude of a wealthy socialite. "Dinner won't be ready for a few more minutes, but you can have a seat here in the den. My husband Randolph should be down in a few minutes, so I'll let Rachel entertain you while I get everything ready."

Oh, great.

I let Richard and Jane walk past me, and wouldn't look them in the eyes. I followed the

four of them into the den, noticing their some-
what formal dress. Both Mrs. Smith and Jane
wore ankle-length skirts and sweaters. *How hot
they have to be,* I thought. *It's spring!* Mr. Smith
and Richard, too. They all wore sweaters!

"Would you like me to turn up the air for
you?" I asked. "Are you hot?"

Mr. Smith planted himself in the big chair,
Dad's chair, and put his feet up. "No, no. We're
fine. We've always liked it a little warm."

Whatever floats your boat, I reasoned to
myself. Then Richard and Jane sat on the floor
at my feet and Mrs. Smith nestled in the
Victorian chair, *Mom's chair.* They all stared at
me, waiting to be entertained. I only knew one
thing to do.

I reached behind me, and switched on the
television.

Richard and Jane instantly started backing
up. Mr. Smith got out of Dad's chair and walked
over to his wife on the far side of the room. She
didn't get up, but looked a little on edge.

"Rachel, dear. Didn't your mother ever tell
you that it's not nice to watch television while
you have company?" Mrs. Smith asked.

"S-Sorry," I said, flipping off the switch.

Now I could rely on nothing but my charm. Searching for a foundation for any conversation, I could only think of one thing to ask.

"Did you ever live overseas?" I asked, directing the question to Mr. Smith, whose sheer presence drew attention away from the others.

"Why, yes, we did," he said, coming back to Dad's chair and sitting down. "For a year when the children were very young."

I turned to Jane, who gave me a cold stare.

"So is that where you learned to eat bugs?" I asked. Jane didn't answer.

"That's right," Mr. Smith cut in. "She and Richard both got a taste for insects. Now they're forever bringing them home and asking Mrs. Smith to prepare them for dinner."

"But I never do," Mrs. Smith continued. "I never liked that cuisine myself, so I'd never be able to make it. I've tried to break the kids of that habit. Now I don't allow bugs in the house at all. Except for the ones already hiding there, of course."

"But Richard said he collects bugs," I said.

Mr. and Mrs. Smith both looked down at Richard, who gave them what I thought was a guilty look.

"I'm sorry, Rachel. It seems you've told us something that we were not aware of," said Mr. Smith.

"We're going to have a discussion when we get home, young man," warned Mrs. Smith. "You know what we've told you about bug collecting."

The room fell silent after that, but only for a few seconds. Mom came into the room.

"Dinner is served," she announced.

Sitting down at the table, I couldn't help feeling bad about getting Richard in trouble. *Sure, he's weird, but if I'm a squealer, that doesn't make me any better,* I believed. So I sat beside him, hoping that during the course of the meal he would let me know there weren't any hard feelings. He remained quiet, however, as did Jane. Only the adults were talking.

Dad had come down and introduced himself in his usual outgoing way. He got along great with people. So did Mom, which led me to believe I was adopted.

"You're antisocial, aren't you?" asked Richard right out of the blue, as Mom brought the spaghetti sauce to the table.

"Huh? What are you talking about?" I asked him, shocked by the question.

"You don't like talking to people. You'd rather be off playing by yourself," Jane chimed in.

I suddenly wanted to punch them both. *HOW DARE THEY!* I couldn't believe it! Coming into my house for dinner and calling me antisocial!

"That doesn't mean I'm antisocial," I said angrily.

The adults stopped their conversation and looked at me. My heart rate shot up a few notches, and I could feel my breathing get heavy.

"Do you have many friends?" Jane asked.

I started to answer, but then Richard cut in—"Are you very popular in school?"

For some reason, my brain froze up. My mouth received no signals to move. I just sat there, horrified by the questions I desperately didn't want to answer in front of an audience.

"Cheerleaders are very popular," Mom jumped in. "Rachel tried out for the squad Friday. We're very confident she'll make the squad."

"When do you find out if you made it, Rachel?" Mrs. Smith asked.

"Tomorrow afternoon," I said, glaring at the monster Smith children. Who did they think they were, questioning my personality? They had as much warmth and cheer as two root canals.

Then my dad, who seemed a lot friendlier than he had when he got home, started the chatter anew.

"So what kind of business are you in, Tom?" he asked. "And please call me Randy. Randolph's a little too formal for me!"

"I deal in plants, Randy," he said.

My stomach bottomed out. *Plants?!*

"Plants?" my dad asked.

"Yes. I'm what you might call a flora and fauna arranger," answered Mr. Smith. "I place certain kinds of plants where people want them. Here's an example. A large company may want plants on every floor of their new office tower. I come in and figure out what kind of plants should go where, based on the light and space available. Then I arrange for it to be completed. It's quite lucrative."

"Wow, a plant person," my dad said with awe. "Now that must be a relaxing job. I'm an accountant, myself. I'm always flying around, and never really have any time for things. Hey! You know what you could do? You could come into my office and plant some flowers right next to my desk. Then no matter how busy I get, I could stop, bend down, and smell them."

A joke. Dad made a very bad joke.

Mr. Smith stared him in the eyes, searching I think, for some kind of sign. Then he burst out laughing.

"Randy, you have a great sense of humor!" he exclaimed, and the two laughed it up.

"That would be great," Mom said. "The only time Randolph bends down at work these days is to get a donut from the bottom drawer of his desk."

Mrs. Smith gave my mom the same stare Mr. Smith had shown my dad, and then she, too, started laughing. The contagious chuckling spread to my mother, and everyone was laughing except me and the solemn duo.

Richard picked all of the meatballs from his spaghetti and chewed them up feverishly. Jane did the same. Then I noticed that their parents, too, had also scarfed down their meatballs.

"Do you have any more meat?" Richard asked loudly to my mother.

My mother stopped laughing at Dad's latest quip so she could hear. "I'm sorry, dear, I didn't hear you."

"I said, do you have any more meat?"

"Any meat?" my mom questioned.

I couldn't believe the gall of that little brat. I thought his sister had no manners, but he took the cake! I sat back and waited for his parents to jump on his case again.

But they never did. Instead, Dad spoke up. "Honey, don't we have some leftover hamburgers from last night in the fridge?"

"Yes," she said slowly, totally puzzled. "We sure do."

As Mom got up from the table to get the burgers, Jane asked, "May I have one, too?"

"Sure," Mom said, moving toward the kitchen.

"You know, Patty, I think I'll have one of those, too," said Mrs. Smith.

Mom turned to Mr. Smith. "How about you, Tom?"

"Thank you, Patty. I sure will," he answered.

Dad started grinning. "I hear you, Tom. When I sit down to a plateful of noodles, I just don't ever get up satisfied. I'm a meat-and-potatoes man, just like you."

"Forget the potatoes," Mr. Smith said. "Just give me the meat."

The whole table began chuckling, even Richard and Jane. I didn't get the joke, and suddenly, I wasn't very hungry.

9

The Smiths left around ten o'clock that night. Before I could hit the stairs and head for my room, Mom drafted me into helping her wash the dishes. To my surprise, Dad even helped clear off the table.

"Remember for the menu next time, Patty, no noodles. Or vegetables, either. That family won't eat them," Dad said, bouncing into the kitchen and placing the plates beside the sink. He was dancing around like some old timer on *American Bandstand*.

"You're telling me?!" Mom answered, handing me a plate to dry. "I had to heat up that frozen meatloaf from two weeks ago. And they even ate the hot dogs without buns! But they're great people, though, don't you think?"

"I think they're cool," Dad replied, dancing the last of the plates into the kitchen. His groove soon became Mom's, too, and they both began to boogie around to some bad disco.

They were making me sick. I resolved to do the dishes as quickly as possible and get out of there. Reaching for another sponge from Mom's side, I caught a whiff of her shirt sleeve.

That smell.

"What's the matter, honey?" Mom asked.

"You stink," I said. "You're covered with some kind of odor."

"What's it smell like?" she asked.

"It's kind of hard to describe. Sort of like sweet sulfur, I guess," I told her.

"Well, thank you, dear. I appreciate that very much. I can finish up here, okay? You need to get to bed," she said sarcastically, taking the soapy sponge from my hand and turning back to the sink. "And I need to go take a bath."

I didn't want to get out of my chores by insulting Mom, but the damage had been done. I took advantage of it and crept out of the kitchen and up the stairs.

Where could that smell be coming from? I wondered. *And why am I the only one smelling it?* I figured it had to be coming from the Smiths. I'd only smelled that scent twice; once with Richard and Jane and the other time near their house, the day I encountered those plants.

I got ready for bed, then spent twenty minutes reading a new plant article before switching off my lamp.

Just before I closed my eyes, I heard a door slam outside. It came from the Smith house.

Someone came out their back door. There were no porch lights on anywhere, but in the moonlight I could see who it was. In the next few seconds, the mystery deepened.

Richard Smith stepped quietly down his driveway with a shovel in his hand. He wore dark clothes now, and looked cautiously in every direction. Soon, he disappeared out of sight.

I checked the clock. Eleven on the nose. No parent would let their kids out that late. I decided to stay up and see when Richard would come back.

10

I didn't get much sleep that night.

I finally dozed off somewhere around three o'clock. Richard hadn't shown up by then. I was pretty groggy when I woke up.

As I looked out the window, I had to squint to protect my eyes against an unforgiving morning sun. Then a weird thing happened which made me force my eyes to open wider.

The plant piece, the one that I kept in the jar, looked like it was moving again. It seemed to be making little scratches against the side of the glass.

I got up for a closer look, and as I got to the window sill, I noticed something moving at the Smith's house.

Richard! He still had the shovel—he was just returning to his house!

I looked back down to the plant, and it

stopped moving. I decided to store it where I could keep an eye on it, so I dropped it into my backpack.

The rest of my morning seemed like snapshots. Rachel almost washes her face completely off with a cold rag to wake herself up, Rachel falls asleep right beside her morning muffin, Rachel gets hit in head by a paper wad while sleeping on the bus, and finally, Rachel gets reprimanded in her first three classes for snoring.

Then I made it to lunch, where I counted on getting a chocolate milk and some vitamin-packed grub to wake me up. I almost jumped for joy when I read the menu.

Pizza day. My favorite day of all.

I got my steaming plate and entered the cafeteria, a vast ocean of motion. Making my way to my regular table, I grinned slightly when I saw it half empty. No one would be there to interrupt me today. *Good,* I thought, *I want to take another look at this plant.*

Sitting down, I took the plant from my backpack, looking closely inside the jar to see if it was moving. Nothing. So I decided to eat, placing the jar on the table just for a second. I got one bite out of my pizza before the two chairs beside me were pulled out from the table and then filled with bodies.

Richard and Jane.

"What are you doing?" I asked.

"We're sitting down to eat our lunch," said Richard. He looked at my pizza. "Are you going to eat the meat off of that?"

"Yes, I am," I answered.

"What's that?" Richard asked, pointing to the jar.

"Just something," I told him, grabbing the plant's container to put it back in my backpack.

"Let me see it," said Richard, and with lightning speed grabbed the jar from my hand.

"WHAT ARE YOU DOING?" I demanded loudly.

Richard held the jar in his hands, peering through the glass at the tiny seedling inside.

"GIVE IT BACK!" I yelled at him, but then stopped before I could say anything else.

I saw something . . . strange. It looked, just for an instant, like Richard's hands glowed. I couldn't be sure of it, but at the same time it seemed to get slightly warmer around me. It made me feel feverish, and suddenly I didn't want Richard or Jane near me ever again.

I yanked the jar from Richard's hands.

"Will you please leave? I don't like you. Either one of you. Find another table."

"What table should we find?" asked Jane.

"I don't care," I told them. "*Any* other table than this. Go sit with Morgan Taylor. He's kind of weird, just like you. Or go sit with Kyle Banner. He'll love having you. Or how about Gordon Myers and Karen Warner over there? They're pretty popular."

Before I could say another word, the two got up and made their way over to Gordon and Karen's table. I watched them introduce themselves, shake hands, and then, to my surprise, Gordon and Karen offered them seats at their table!

For the rest of lunch, I watched Richard and Jane laugh it up with the two most popular kids in school. They said more to Gordon and Karen in one lunch than I had in four years. And after they finished eating, *the four got up and walked out together.*

Where did the grim twins suddenly get their communication skills from? I asked myself.

I couldn't keep my mind off of it as I sat through my last three classes.

Gym, my last class, started out normally enough. I still felt groggy from getting so little sleep, so I dragged, getting ready after all the other kids. And, par for the course, the last person to leave the locker room forgot I was in there and switched off the light. If it wasn't for the sun coming through tiny upper-wall windows, I couldn't have seen anything.

"Thanks! Really appreciate it," I said to an empty room. *This always happens*, I griped in my head. *Am I really that invisible?*

Then suddenly, Mr. Trout, our principal, came on the intercom.

"I have the results of the cheerleader tryouts," he said.

CHEERLEADER TRYOUTS! I couldn't believe I'd forgotten . . .

POP.

A sound . . . *coming from my stuff on the floor*. Like a hole being punched in . . . metal.

Then something moved in my backpack.

I stayed still and waited for it to repeat itself.

It did.

Reaching slowly over to the pack, I carefully unstripped the Velcro. Holding my breath, I lifted the flap.

Curling in and out like worms, the plant piece had come to life and burst out of the little glass container.

I flipped the flap back over, but not before one of the plant's newly grown vines had wrapped around my wrist.

"Karen Warner . . . " Principal Trout read through the names as I pulled my hand away, balled up the backpack and threw it in my locker. I stood there, pressing my hands against the door just in case it tried to get out.

"And the last cheerleader for our next year's Timberwolf squad will be . . ."

"... Rachel Pearson."

Just as Mr. Trout said my name, the vines came through the locker vent, reaching out to grab me.

I jumped back, tripping over the bench behind me and falling backwards to the floor. Like snakes, the vines spread over the face of the lockers, down to the floor, and then started crawling across the room.

Just as they got close to me, I got to my feet. Screaming my lungs out, I ran to the door, only to be met by the green tentacles as they flipped the door lock.

I kept screaming for help and ran to the other exit that led outside. That's when it grabbed my ankle.

Instantly, it pulled me to the floor and began

to drag me. I kicked and stomped, while grabbing at anything that would anchor me. The benches were bolted to the floor, so I grabbed the leg of one and held on for dear life.

I kept screaming, locking my terrified eyes on the plant tendrils as they yanked at my leg, trying to loosen my grip.

Then to my horror, each vine sprouted more tentacles.

They wove themselves up my leg, covering it like a web. The tiny sprouts took hold of each part of my body, until finally making their way to my head.

First, they put an end to my screaming by covering my mouth, then they wrapped themselves around my eyes. I couldn't see, and could hardly breathe, using only my nose to suck in oxygen.

Finally, the vines went for my right hand, which held the bench leg with such a vise-like grip that it would have taken ten men to pry it loose. The vines did it in seconds. They covered my hand, then sprouted new, tinier tentacles to creep under my fingers and push them loose.

Suddenly, I felt myself moving across the floor again.

The vines pulled me around the corner of the lockers and past the door.

I heard banging on the other side.

They heard my screams, I rationalized through my terror. *Please! Please save me!*

The vines slipped from my face a little, and I could finally see out of one eye. At the door, more tendrils crawled up the frame, fortifying a barricade that couldn't be broken through.

I tried to scream, but the vines crept down my throat, gagging me and making my eyes water. Through blurred vision, I saw where it was pulling me.

My locker. As it dragged me closer, I found out why, and starting thrashing about with every bit of strength I had.

The plant had become a monster. What used to be a tiny green shell was now a huge mouth. It had grown, taking the shape of an egg on its side, and splitting it right down the center were rows of razor-sharp teeth. It slobbered, and the warm, thick saliva hit my arm and my legs as it dragged me to the base of my locker. It started to pull me up to its frothing jaws.

With every bit of strength I had, I wrestled my arm free, grabbed my shoe from the floor, and threw it right at the plant's mouth. It simply caught the shoe in its teeth, and shook it around like a rag, before tossing it to the floor. I picked up my other shoe and did the same thing. This time the vines loosened the their grip just enough for me to break free.

Hitting the floor, I scrambled straight for the door. I got halfway there before the vines wrapped around me again, jerking me back like a yo-yo. My feet went up into the air and hit the light switch, turning them on.

Suddenly the vines let go of me. I rolled over in time to see the plant's tentacles recoil into my locker. The last one to make it in shut the door.

Gasping for air, I watched to make sure the monster didn't spring out again and come after me. My mind tried to pull itself together, but hardly anything registered.

It didn't eat you, is all I could muster. *It didn't eat you.*

The banging on the locker-room door suddenly cut through the cobwebs in my brain, and I heard the coach's voice.

"PEARSON! OPEN THIS DOOR NOW! DO YOU HEAR ME?"

Her voice thundered in my head as I wearily got to my feet. Staring at the spot, I reached over and flicked off the lights.

Once again, the vines began to creep slowly out of my locker.

I turned the lights back on.

The vines retracted, pulling themselves back into their dark cave.

The lights. It can't stand these lights, I told myself.

"RACHEL! FOR THE LAST TIME OPEN THIS DOOR!" yelled the coach.

Rational thoughts started returning to me. I moved shakily to open the door.

Then something exploded behind me.

I instinctively jumped to a corner to hide, covering my head with my hands while letting out a horrible shriek. Something banged very loudly, but after a few seconds I realized nothing was going to attack me.

I moved from the corner and warily peeked around the lockers to see if the monster had come out.

The door to my locker was bent forward at a right angle and toward the floor. The other exit door to the locker room slowly swung closed.

The monster had escaped.

As the coach made her final threat from the other side of the door, I wondered how I would explain any of this.

12

In the course of ten minutes, I went from being the invisible student to being the center of attention for the entire gym class.

I let the coach in and she examined me thoroughly. My flustered expression had to be noticeable, but to my surprise the plant had left no visible cuts or bruises. At first, the coach seemed to be concerned for my safety. However, after she checked me out, she started in with the questions.

At that moment, I couldn't answer a thing—the shock of what had happened had completely drained me, and I felt like fainting.

The coach took me from the locker room, through the crowd of onlooking students, to the school nurse.

I spent at least an hour with the nurse,

crouched sheepishly in a chair, sipping orange juice. Then the principal came in and asked me what happened.

All I could get out was, "Can I go home?"

"I want an answer," said Mr. Trout.

"Please," I asked again. "Can I go home?"

"I want to know who ripped that locker door off, and I want to know what you were screaming about," he said.

"A plant monster," I said sheepishly.

He stared at me for a long moment, before finally saying, "I'm calling your parents."

As he walked from the room I realized that seeing is believing. Since I happened to be the only person attacked by the monster, I would be the only person who believed in the monster. Otherwise, it just sounded like a bunch of baloney. To the rest of the world, plant monsters didn't exist.

Thirty minutes later, Mr. Trout re-entered the room with my neighbor, Sheriff Drake.

"Rachel," Mr. Trout said. "I've tried calling your mother and father at work, but neither one of them can be reached. I contacted Sheriff Drake here, and he's going to take you home. But rest assured, young lady, this matter will be investigated, and if need be, disciplinary action will be taken. You might just find your spot on the cheerleading squad open next year."

On the way out, I almost chuckled over Mr. Trout's last comments. Ever since the announcement, I hadn't even given a thought to making the cheerleading squad. Besides that, after what I'd just been through, threats to take that position away seemed laughable.

I didn't share those thoughts with Sheriff Drake. I didn't share much with him at all, even though he questioned me all the way home. When we got to my house, he watched from the car as I unlocked the door and started inside. I turned and waved goodbye to him, although I got the feeling he might hang around for a few minutes.

Whatever. I didn't care. I went straight up to my room, collapsed on my bed, and went into a deep sleep.

It wasn't a pleasant one.

I woke up screaming at about seven o'clock that night, throwing my sheets to the floor and clutching my pillow as my only shield of defense. Sweat beaded off my forehead, and my heart pounded. I caught my breath, and waited for

Mom to come in, wanting to know what that scream was about. To my surprise, the door never opened.

The phone rang. I let it ring six times before I picked it up.

"H-Hello?" I asked.

"Rachel? Rachel Pearson?" a girl's voice asked from the other end of the line.

"Yes?" I warily replied.

"Hi! This is Libb Randall, your fellow cheerleader. I'm calling to see if you're okay," she said in a semi-genuinely concerned voice.

"Yeah, I'm okay," I told her, pulling my blanket from the floor and wrapping it around myself.

"Everyone wants to know what went on with you today! People are starting to make up stories, but I figured I'd call you and get the real scoop," she said.

"Libb, I'm really not feeling well . . ."

"Oh, I'm sorry," Libb replied. "I'll let you go. But I wanted to let you know that I'm having a party tomorrow for our newly elected squad! I know you're sick, so don't feel bad if you can't come. You've probably got the same thing as Karen. She can't make it either."

Bells rang in my head.

"Karen Warner?" I asked. "She's sick?"

"Yeah," Libb answered. "Some kind of flu, I think. I just talked to her mother. She went to that new girl's house after school and started feeling bad while she was there. When she got home she was running a fever of a hundred and one."

I couldn't believe it. Things were getting out of control.

"Libb, you're good friends with Gordon Myers, aren't you?" I asked.

"Oh, yeah. Best friends," she answered.

"Can I get his phone number from you?"

"Well, sure," she said. "But I think you're wasting your time. He and Karen have been spending a lot of time together. As a matter of fact, he's sick, too."

"WHAT?" I almost yelled. My suspicions were being confirmed.

"Yeah. His mom called to congratulate me a while ago and told me," she explained. "I guess this flu's really going around."

I felt my whole body sag, and I slumped to the floor.

"Libb, I'll call you back later," I said.

Hanging up the phone, I slowly made my way out of my room and down the stairs. I had to tell Mom and Dad what had happened. *I'd make them believe me.*

They had to stay away from the Smith family. Those kids of theirs had made Gordon and Karen sick. I totally believed that. I also believed that Richard did something to that plant. He'd made it come to life, and I was sure he could do it again.

An uneasy feeling came over me when I found the house empty downstairs. Walking into the kitchen, I flipped the light on, revealing a note stuck to the refrigerator.

"Spent the day with the Smiths. We're also having dinner there. Come over when you get home—Love, Mom and Dad."

Spent the day at the Smith's?

They didn't go to work?

What were they thinking? How could they . . .

Then it hit me . . .

The Smiths had them. They'd lured my parents over there, and Mom and Dad had no clue what was going on.

Just as that thought sank in, there was a knock at my door.

Mom and Dad!

Without thinking, I ran to the door and yanked it open.

Richard and Jane stood there on my front porch, smiling.

"Hello, Rachel," they said in unison.

"STAY AWAY!" I cried, slamming the door shut and locking it.

I ran to the phone and dialed 9-1-1 faster than I could breathe.

No dial tone.

"Aw, come on, Rachel!" yelled Richard from the other side of the door. "You're not going to get away here! We cut the phone lines already!"

Dropping the phone, I darted to the back door. Locked.

Every entrance to the house appeared in my mind. I'd have to check them all.

Running into the dining room, I switched on the light. No windows in there. I moved to the den. One by one, I switched on every lamp, then cautiously made my way over to the windows.

My hands were sweating so much I had to

grip the curtain pull with both of them. Every muscle in my body tensed as I pulled the curtain, slowly at first, then, unable to stand it, *I jerked them open with one quick pull.*

I didn't see anything.

I backed away, keeping my eyes on the glass the whole time, until I bumped into the stereo.

An idea crossed my mind. I switched on the stereo and moved the dial to the loudest rock station I could find, and cranked it up.

That will bring the neighbors running, I thought. *Now to check the upstairs windows.*

I climbed the stairs sideways with my back against the wall. I'd be ready to run in case the Smith kids popped out of nowhere. When I got to the top, I ducked to the right into Mom and Dad's room and flipped on the light.

Empty. I'd half-hoped my parents would be taking a nap there, so I could wake them up to protect me. *But the Smith family already had them.*

I moved to the window, and my heart stopped when I saw the shade flutter ever so slightly. I held my breath, reached over, and drew it up.

Again, nothing there, but the window stood

open. I moved like lightning and shut it, locking it in less than a second.

Two more rooms to go, I told myself. My throat pounded because my heart had moved up into it, and my nerves seemed to sense every speck of dust that touched my skin. I had no idea where they were. They could already be in the house and I might not know it.

I thought I saw a shadow move when I got to the edge of the guest room. The rock music blared so loudly I couldn't hear anything else, but I trusted my eyes. Grabbing an umbrella from the hall corner, I reached into the room with it and flipped on the light.

THERE! RIGHT AT THE WINDOW! ONE OF THEM!

NO, no . . . it was just my mother's plant, Fred. She'd put it there last week. But I still had to check the windows. I ran in and checked the first window. *Closed and locked.* Then I saw Fred's leaves blowing back and forth. I jumped to the next window and slammed it shut, knocking Fred to the floor in the process. Dirt covered the carpet, but I ran right through it to get out of the room.

Only my room left.

By now, every light in the house was on except my own. I flipped the switch and entered the room.

What am I looking for? I asked myself. *I never open my window. My room's definitely secure.*

Then the music stopped.

One by one, every light in the house blinked off.

14

"We're in the house, Rachel," came Jane's voice. "And we're going to get you."

"LEAVE ME ALONE!" I shrieked, backing into a corner.

"We can't do that. You know things we can't let get out!" Richard's voice echoed through the house.

"I DON'T KNOW ANYTHING! LET ME GO!" My voice became a pleading sob. My body shook uncontrollably, and I fell to my knees in the face of their terror.

"Rachel, Rachel, Rachel. We know you have suspicions. We'll end those suspicions," said Jane.

"DON'T HURT ME!" I pleaded.

"We don't have to hurt you. That's the greatest part. We can simply make you forget. We'll take a little piece of your brain, and you'll forget you were ever scared! Now isn't that cool of us?" asked Richard.

I found myself begging to the darkness, asking voices in the air to be merciful to me. But I didn't believe him one bit.

"YOU EAT MEAT!" I screamed.

"Give the girl a prize," said Richard.

"Yes, Rachel, we do eat meat. We can't eat vegetables, now, can we? We're not cannibals. And the bugs, they're really just for snacking. But if you want to feel nice and full, there's nothing better than a big hunk of meat. So here's the deal. We make you forget all about us now, and when we finally do eat you, you'll never see it coming!" Jane said, with a slight chuckle.

I had to get out of there. The drop from my window had to be at least twenty feet. If I landed right, I'd live to run to Sheriff Drake's house.

Hopping on my bed, I unlocked the window and pushed it open.

"Game time," I heard Richard's voice say from behind me.

They were in my room.

15

I felt something wrap around my waist and squeeze. A vine, just like the one that had attacked me in the locker room.

"NO! LEAVE ME ALONE!" I screamed.

"Why don't you want to hang with us?" Jane asked.

"Yeah, you've got to admit, we're a lot more fun now," said Richard. "See, we just took a little personality from both Gordon and Karen, clouded their memories, and they're no worse for the wear. Now we have the tools to blend in. We don't sound so stiff, so weird."

"We would have come to you first, Rachel, but you don't seem to have a personality everybody loves. Why, until today, no one even knew you were alive," said Jane.

The moonlight filled my room enough for me

to see the vine. It kept getting tighter. They had me.

"What did you do to Mom and Dad?" I sobbed, my voice hoarse from screaming.

"Mr. and Mrs. Smith are taking care of them," explained Richard. "Last night they sprayed your parents with some of the . . . chemicals that our bodies use. Sort of like how a skunk sprays you with its stink, y'know? Anyway, the stuff makes you do whatever we want, for a little while, of course. I tried spraying you the other day on the hill, but you took off too fast, you little jerk. Now, come on, Rachel, aren't you at least going to turn around and deal with us face to face?"

My body quaked so badly that I couldn't be sure of what it would do next. I turned slowly to have a look at what I thought might be the last sight I ever saw.

Before long, I only wished it had been.

Standing in the moonlight from the window, they both looked normal at first. However, the smiles that crossed their faces gave away their eagerness. I realized too late something terrifying was about to happen.

Their heads split right down the middle.

"AGGGHHH!" I screamed, louder than I thought possible, as the unnatural sight unfolded before me.

Like sliced melons being pulled apart, their heads opened vertically, and a clear, thick gel sprayed over the room. As if a nestful of snakes had awakened, tentacles coiled out from the center of each head, wriggling into the air. They searched for their prey.

Me.

The noises bursting from my lungs didn't sound like screams anymore. Caterwauls would be closest to describing them. The shrieks poured out of me as the vines slithered from my neighbors' heads and wrapped around me.

I completely lost it. My body moved with more power and speed than I knew I had, jetting between the two Smith children and out the door. The vines tightened their grip and almost stopped me . . .

But not before I went over the staircase.

When I fell, the tentacles jerked tight. I hung there for a second and then pulled Richard and Jane over with me.

16

We landed hard.

My fall had been slowed, but it still knocked the wind out of me.

Richard and Jane plummeted to the carpet, crashing around me with unforgiving momentum. Again, the clear gel sprayed into the air, dotting my face and getting into my eye. Half of Richard landed on my leg, and Jane plunged into Dad's chair.

No one moved. We just lay there in the darkness.

My eyes stayed open and I could make out the stray vines crawling about on the floor, but none of them attacked me. It seemed safer to lie still, and not draw attention to myself. But when I saw the door out of the corner of my eye, I knew I needed to move.

Pulling my leg out from under the monstrosity that used to be Richard, I rose slowly to my feet, then darted for the door.

I didn't even make it halfway.

Jane's entire body had opened up into a flowering bud, producing tendrils from every pore. They snaked around me and pulled me into the living room, where I quickly lost my balance, slamming to the floor just in front of the fireplace.

When I opened my eyes, I saw the butane lighter my dad had bought to light fires with, sitting just a few inches away on the hearth.

Pulling my arm free, I grabbed the lighter and flicked it on, illuminating a small portion of the dark room. Then I held it to the tentacles that bound me.

"AAAAACCCCCKKKK!" shrieked the monster Jane from some unseen mouth.

The vines retracted from around me, and I scrambled to my feet.

Richard had recovered from the fall and moved to the entry, blocking my escape. I held up the lighter as a weapon, keeping both of them away from me.

"You'll never get out of here! We'll eat you if

we must!" Richard growled.

"STAY AWAY!" I warned. "You're not going to eat anybody! I'll burn you first! I'll get Sheriff Drake! He'll help me end this whole thing and get my parents back!"

"This thing's not going to end," snarled Jane, mutating into something larger. "There are more of us coming! By the time you get anyone to believe you, they'll be here!"

"You're lying!" I shouted, pointing the small flame her way. They couldn't make me listen to them anymore.

"I planted an army of them last night! Mr. Smith intends to greet them when they rise this evening. You're already too late!" bragged Richard.

I couldn't keep them away forever. As I searched for a way out, I spotted the open fuse box behind Jane's mass. That's how they'd shut off the lights. I crept my way over to the television, remembering two things. The first was how the entire Smith family had shrunk away from the television when I turned it on. The second was how Dad swore he'd never miss another episode of *Pierwatch* after Mom blew a fuse using the hair dryer. He ran the television through another circuit outside, and I prayed the monsters hadn't thrown that switch, too.

I reached for it, and with a flip of the knob the television came on.

The entire room was washed in bouncing blue light, and Richard and Jane began to whine and stiffen up. The light from the television seemed to be killing them.

Warm lights won't hurt them, I thought. *But fluorescent lighting . . . it'll get them every time.*

I took advantage of the distraction. Richard still blocked the entryway, but in his weakened state, I was able to push him aside. Jetting through the dining room and into the kitchen, I quickly unbolted the lock on the back door.

I heard Richard and Jane roar to life behind me.

I flung the door open and jumped out, but not before a tentacle wrapped around me. Out of reflex, I whipped around and shoved the lit burner into whatever came up behind me.

Richard's bulbous, dripping head.

Whatever the clear goo they leaked happened to be, it was flammable. The monster boy's head lit up like a bonfire.

Jane couldn't stop her advance and plowed right into her flailing brother, sending them both soaring out to the porch.

They hit the ground and rolled. Their limbs tried to find leverage to rise, causing them to interweave and curl inside and out like layers of live wire.

Thank goodness the fire spread quickly!

Eruptions of liquid spewed forth from every part of their bodies, followed by gas discharges from underneath them. Their shells bubbled into liquid as their own vines tried desperately to get away.

I climbed the hill behind my house to get out of the way. When I looked back, the two had become something like green, oozing marshmallows. Their screams died out into one horrible moan.

I turned around, kept climbing, and didn't look back again.

17

My mind raced with choices.

I've got to get Sheriff Drake! But what about Mom and Dad? Are there really more of these things coming?

Even through my scatterbrained panic, common sense told me to find Sheriff Drake. I just wanted to climb up the hill, circle wide, and then run down to the street. I didn't want to get close to my house again, just in case I hadn't seen the last of Richard and Jane.

Before I went into the woods, my injuries had just been a collection of bruises. When I barreled full speed into the trees and bushes, however, the branches and limbs ripped at my skin. I felt the cuts multiplying, but nothing could stop me from getting out of there.

I only stumbled a couple of times before I came to the opposite edge of the brush, dangerously close to the Smith house.

Don't worry, Mom and Dad, I thought, glancing at the lifeless home. *I'll get the Sheriff and we'll get you out of there!*

As I turned my head to look forward again, my eyes met a black wall. I smashed into it and fell to the ground.

Gathering my senses, I looked up, and cried out in terror.

Mr. Smith stood right over me.

18

"Hello, Rachel," he said. "Seen Richard and Jane around lately?"

I didn't know if he really meant it or not, so I started to answer him. Then he reached down, grabbed me by the shirt, and hoisted me into the air. He must have known the answer.

"I suppose you want to see what your mom and dad are up to, huh?" he asked, pulling me right toward his face. His breath smelled of hamburger. "Well, why don't we go into the house and have a nice little family reunion?"

Having said that, he tucked me under his arm like a potato sack and carried me into his yard. He didn't bother with the handle when we got to the door, but just kicked it open instead.

Mrs. Smith appeared in the hall.

"She's still running around?" asked Mrs. Smith.

"Not anymore," said Mr. Smith. "She's come to see her mommy and daddy!"

My body felt like cement. A heavy numbness drained into my arms and legs, multiplying the helpless feelings swirling about in my head. *Doomed. I was doomed.*

"What about Richard and Jane?" she asked with very little emotion.

"They're casualties," said Mr. Smith with no emotion at all.

He strode through the hall, passed Mrs. Smith, and stopped at the door leading to the basement. He kicked that one in, too.

Without turning the light on, he carried me down the stairs. With each step, the realization swept over me that something terrible must have happened to my parents. Even worse, I might be just seconds from experiencing the same fate.

When we reached the bottom stair, Mr. Smith felt along the wall, searching for a light switch.

"Mom? Dad?" Mr. Smith asked out loud. "Rachel's home."

He flipped the light on, and my sobs turned to shrieks.

19

The entire basement was packed with vegetation—it filled every corner and crack in the floor. Enormous pods that looked like large, stubby green beans leaned against every wall, pulsing and dripping with slime. Vines clung from the ceiling, slithering across in defiance of gravity. They dripped liquid, and the floors glistened from the thick, sticky gunk that seemed to leak steadily not only from the vines but from the other plants in the room as well.

Mr. Smith moved forward, sloshing through the gelatinous seepage to reach the hanging ceiling light in the middle of the room.

"Your parents have been worried about you," he said, then grabbed the lamp and pointed it into the darkest corner of the room.

There were Mom and Dad.

I screamed at the horrible sight.

They had been encased in pods. Like giant leeches, the plant things had practically swallowed them whole. The only part of their bodies still showing were their heads, protruding from the tops of the bulbous containers. Tiny tendrils rose up from the pods' ends and attached themselves to various parts of my parents' heads. A thick slime covered their faces, but I could see their closed eyes through the shiny, clear film. The pods themselves seemed to be breathing. They expanded and contracted very delicately, as if my parents were too much to digest at once.

"THEY'RE EATING THEM!" I howled in terror. My muscles sprang to life and I kicked and clawed at Mr. Smith in a desperate attempt to get loose.

I heard him curse just before he heaved me into the air.

I landed right on top of the largest piece of plant mass in the room, and burst right through its skin.

Completely losing it, I shrieked and tried to climb my way out, but the plant gave me nothing to grab on to. The muck inside of it felt like Jell-O, only with a rougher, drier texture. I flung its pasty entrails in every direction. Trying to get to my feet, I ripped at the tight, thin film that served as its skin. Then, just as I got enough leverage to stand up, it used its legs. Eight long, green limbs that looked terrifyingly close to spider legs lifted into the air and closed down on top of me.

"NO! LET ME GO! PLEASE!" I kept begging, but the green beast tightened around me. Its legs caged me in, and I felt its puttylike insides hardening, cementing me in as it lifted me off the floor. It made sickening noises, like a hundred plungers being used at once. Soon it settled, and the sound changed to something like an unclogging drain. The thin skin re-formed itself, leaving only my head sticking out, angled backwards toward the floor. Gooey gel from its closure ran down my neck and dripped off my ears onto the floor. It was eating me.

"IT'S KILLING ME!" I sobbed, tears filling my eyes and running across my face. **"IT'S EATING ME ALIVE!"**

A black shadow crossed my face, taking away the light.

"You're not being eaten," said Mr. Smith as he bent down closer to me. "You're being contained. I can't have any normal people disappearing around this town. Not just yet!"

His words sounded honest. My hopes clung to them, and I prayed he was telling the truth.

"WHAT'S GOING TO HAPPEN TO ME?" I screamed.

Mr. Smith brought his hands into the air, and for a second I thought he would strangle me.

"You're going to keep quiet, you little brat," he warned, then calmed himself. "No harm will come to you or your parents on this night. As I said, I don't want the townsfolk getting suspicious of me just yet. If your family disappeared suddenly, it would bring too many questions."

"W-What have you done to my parents?" I asked as my eyes dried a bit, letting me see his face more clearly. His skin had become bumpy, and tiny branchlike protrusions dotted his face. The whites of his eyes had turned green, and his irises countered by changing from blue to red.

"We've just borrowed a little of their personalities," he explained. "If you remember, we Smiths happened to be a pretty bland group when we got here. We needed to blend in, and it would have taken too long to learn how to correctly use emotion. So we simply tap into it, collecting brain patterns from very outgoing people and recording them into our chemistry. We're very adaptable that way. And your parents? They'll just be a little woozy for a couple of days. No permanent damage at all."

"Then—then, what are you going to do to me?" I asked, knowing Richard and Jane had told me I wasn't needed, and I guessed their parents felt the same.

"We're just going to have you relax and fall

into a deep sleep. I've got some things to do tonight, and I don't need anyone getting in my way," he said, in a way that felt both comforting and dreadful at the same time.

I heard something move across the floor. Dropping my head back and looking straight ahead, I saw a plant mass beginning to blossom into a beautiful violet and pink flower. It opened like a reverse umbrella, showering the air with its pollinating mist. Yellow flakes drifted to the floor, many of them landing on my face. I felt a slight burning as they melted into my skin, entering my bloodstream.

"WHAT IS IT?" I asked, suddenly panicking that Mr. Smith had lied about my safety.

"Just a sleeping aid," he assured me. "Once you've dozed off, my friend over there will remove all of those nasty memories for you." He pointed to one of the pods on the other wall, and the plant raised a vine in the air as if to show me where it was.

I started feeling really warm and a little drowsy. I tried desperately to make sense of things. I didn't want to forget.

"Who are you, really?" I asked, calming considerably with each passing second. "Why are you doing this?"

Mr. Smith got to his feet and peered down at me.

"We're plants," he said, "and we're taking over."

As he left the room, I felt my brain begin to go numb and my eyelids grow heavier.

21

With every bit of willpower I had, I desperately tried not to fall asleep.

I dug one of my fingernails into my thumb to get a steady amount of pain feeding through my senses. The pollen made me so sleepy that I found it hard to keep any single thought in my head. I couldn't focus.

Plant People . . . taking over . . . have to stop them . . . just a kid . . .

One broken message after another filled my mind until they grew fewer and farther between. My neck muscles relaxed, letting my head hang over the floor. My finger stopped digging, and my hand settled back into the hardening ooze of my veggie-prison.

Then the pod across the room began to move. Its vines snaked across the floor, under my head, and latched onto a grate in the corner of the room. The tentacles tightened and began to pull. Falling to the floor with a thud, the giant pod moved slowly across the gunk-coated surface. Its end opened up, and the wormlike, stringy sensors emerged, coiling upright to attention as they honed in on me.

My clouded mind wouldn't let me scream. I lay there, watching it inch its way closer so it could take my memories away. Then I'd be just another oblivious victim when the Plant People took over the town. After I was gone, there would be no one to warn Fairfield.

The thing that held me tightened just slightly, pressing my arm against something in my pocket.

The lighter.

I'd shoved it in my pocket as I escaped from Richard and Jane.

With only a few seconds of coherent thought left, I wiggled my hand into my pocket. I practically dislocated my shoulder as I pulled the burner out, turned it away from my leg, and clicked it on.

Is it on? I wondered through my foggy head. *I can't even see if it's working!*

My only option would be to wait and see.

So I kept my finger pressed on the switch and my eyes locked on the pod as its tendrils slid over my hand, releasing the same gel that covered the faces of Mom and Dad.

Please work, I begged. *Pleeeease work.*

Suddenly, my prison began to shake.

I looked to its right side and saw a fast-growing black spot emerging, with a slight wisp of smoke appearing on its skin.

Then its entire side exploded.

With a gurgling snarl, the plant-prison violently spasmed, extending its legs into the air.

I shot my hand through the hole, then brought it around, ripping the plant open wide enough for me to hop out.

The tentacles on my head tightened, trying to thwart my escape, but I tore them from their base. The pod howled in agony, summoning its scattered, viny arms to attack.

One of them wrapped around my foot and yanked me to the floor. My finger pulled the burner switch by reflex, and I swung it around to light the vine. Like a fuse, the flame zoomed up its length and totally engulfed the pod. It rolled in agony across the floor, dangerously close to

Mom and Dad.

I almost screamed, seeing my parents trapped helplessly as the burning vegetation rolled toward them.

Leaping over the various plants that moved in to grab me, I made my way around the flaming pod and dug my hands into both Mom's and Dad's shell-prisons. Ripping away layer after layer, I dared not take even a second to turn and look at the danger behind me. Only after I pulled my father's arm free of his shell did I take a quick glance at the pod behind me.

It had stopped rolling, but the flames began to spread quickly, and the plants around it started catching fire, too.

Maniacally, I pulled at Dad until the encasement gave way and he fell on top of me. Using more strength than I thought I had, I transferred his weight, pushing him up against the wall to rest while I freed Mom.

Her pod was ready for me. Its tendrils wrapped around my hands, trying to prevent me from tearing into it any further.

But I wouldn't be stopped. I kept digging, yanking the tendrils from their ends and making the pod scream as my hands finally clasped Mom.

Gritting my teeth, I yanked her out. Her weight surprised me. I slipped on the soaked floor, and we both crashed to the ground. As soon as I hit, I felt the rush of heat sting my face. The flames burned just inches away, spreading by the second.

"DAD! HELP ME!" I cried.

He heard me. I knew it as soon as he moved. The plant hadn't killed him, but he looked terrible. He moved slowly, turning to Mom and me. In his cloudiness, he finally seemed to assess the situation and lumbered toward us. Dad lifted Mom from the floor and I shot up right after her.

The fire had almost surrounded us.

A narrow opening looked to be the last way out, and I physically pushed Mom and Dad through it. Dad almost lost his balance, but stayed standing, carrying himself and Mom to safety. I darted through right after them, and followed them up the stairs.

When we got to the door, we found it locked.

I looked to my parents for options, but they were practically brain-dead. I couldn't be sure what the plants had done to them, but now they were acting like zombies. I realized it would be up to me to get all of us out of there.

I clutched the doorknob again, looking for the strength to pull it open.

Then to my amazement, the knob flew from my hands and the door was opened for me.

"WHAT HAVE YOU DONE?!" demanded Mrs. Smith. Her eyes locked on to mine and I knew our escape had been foiled.

22

Every hair on my body stood on end, and my bones shook uncontrollably. Something in my brain snapped.

I leaped like a lion, ramming Mrs. Smith and knocking her into the hallway, hitting the wall.

"MOM! DAD! RUN!" I screamed as my hands and feet wrestled with the she-monster.

My parents heard me and staggered out into the hall, moving slowly for the door. They would never make it unless I could keep Mrs. Smith away from them.

Like a gunslinger, I reached for my weapon, hoping the lighter still had enough fluid to burn Mrs. Smith to the ground. As I lifted it, something hard smashed into my arm, sending the lighter flying down the basement stairs. Then I felt a sharp object pierce the skin of my leg, and I howled in pain. Falling to the floor, I glared at Mrs. Smith.

She had changed.

Where once there had been skin, there was now thick, rough tree bark. She still had human eyes and a human mouth, but the rest of her had mutated into a grey husk. On her leg, I saw what appeared to be a giant thorn with my blood on its tip. It receded back into her thigh, but then I noticed more thorns growing from the tips of her fingers.

"Your reign of terror is about to end, Rachel," she said in a gravelly voice as she rose. "But first, let's punish your parents for raising such a little monster."

She raised her hand to point toward them, and the fingers began to spasm and swell up like they were about to . . . discharge.

"NO!" I yelled, hopping to my feet and charging down the hall for Mom and Dad. They were halfway out the entrance, completely oblivious to what was going on around them. The door started closing slowly behind them, but they would never make it unless . . .

Rocketing for the door, I smashed into it,

sending it crashing into my parents, launching them into the front yard.

Hitting the floor hard, I knew full well I'd just closed off my best exit.

I scrambled to my feet just as five spearlike thorns embedded themselves into the door behind me.

When I reached for the doorknob, Mrs. Smith's crusty arm stretched down the hallway, dug into the door, and held it in place.

"Now it's just me and you," she cackled, and moved in for the kill.

23

The flames from the basement shot up into the hallway behind Mrs. Smith as she came closer.

"You almost ruined everything, Rachel! But we can get a new house! We can grow more kids! What matters is that more of us will be grown, and there's nothing you can do to stop us!"

At the moment, I didn't care about stopping anything. I just wanted to get out of there. As more thorns rose out of Mrs. Smith's shell, my eyes darted desperately from side to side, trying to decide which way to run.

I was in this house even before they were! Where was the other exit? My mind raced for the answer. *The garage!*

I cut to the right, running through the dining room. Thorns laid waste to the walls like bullets from a machine gun. I outran them, making my way to the kitchen. Just as I went through the hall, I hung a right, remembering where the garage was. As I did, Mrs. Smith's arm, now the size of a tree trunk, blasted its way into the room like a locomotive. It missed me by inches, crashing into the refrigerator on the kitchen's far side. It stuck there, and I heard her grunt as she struggled to free it.

I went for the garage.

Another locked door. As luck would have it, it was one of those locks you have to wrestle with before you finally get it open.

My hands moved at a frantic pace, twisting the lock all the way around in hope of finding the right spot.

I heard the twisting metal of the refrigerator as Mrs. Smith's arm began to shrink and retract into itself. She'd be on me in seconds.

Then I heard a click.

Unlocked. Time to go!

I stepped into the garage, slamming the door behind me, only to find more bad news.

The big rollup door was closed.

Darkness filled the entire garage. I couldn't see to find the door switch. I ran my hands along the walls, frantically searching for the controls.

When Mrs. Smith burst through the door, I tried to run to the other side, only to smack right into their minivan. Reeling from the impact, I managed to circle to the other side for cover.

"YOU DENTED OUR MINIVAN!" she cried, showering the entire garage with thorns.

I hid behind the van, curled up in a ball. I knew if I moved an inch one of those things would hit me. My only hope was that she would run out of them soon.

Then one of the thorns struck a metal panel on the wall. A red light came on, and the garage door began to open.

The open night greeted my eyes with a flash of lightning. *Was I fast enough to run for it? Could I make it out before one those thorns planted itself in my head?*

"I'll just have to shut that!" Mrs. Smith growled, and then fired again and again at the control panel. Striking it the first time must have been a lucky shot. She couldn't repeat herself, *and that made her mad.*

She snarled in rage and with her giant trunk

of an arm swung across the entire width of the garage.

Her arm swung *through* the minivan, bringing a shower of glass and metal to the floor. Her hand scraped across the wall, knocking down shelves and tools that hung from them and sending them flying outside the garage.

I'd ducked under the van to avoid being smothered in the wreckage, but I knew I'd have to move when I saw the garage door start to go down again. I rolled out slowly, careful not to cut myself on any of the falling debris. Then I got into position and bounded for the doorway.

The top half of Mrs. Smith's wood-skinned body stretched after me, and she used her smaller hand to grab my foot just as I slipped under the closing door.

It came down right on top of her midsection, but she still hung on to me. Her head and arm stuck out from under it. She had a death grip on my ankle.

"COME BACK INSIDE, RACHEL! BE NEIGHBORLY!" she yelled, as the thorns jutted from her fingers to pierce my skin.

I could see Mom and Dad staggering into the street in front of the house. I screamed, but they wouldn't snap out of it.

I kicked at her head in an attempt to escape, but she just kept laughing. With my arms, I tried pushing away, and then felt something sharp under my hand.

One of the tools she had knocked off the wall.

A hatchet.

I grabbed it, and almost snapped my back lifting it into the air.

My eyes tried to meet Mrs. Smith's gaze, but she morphed, sprouting limbs from her head that curled through the air. She no longer had a face. In fact, she hardly had any resemblance to a human now, except that I could still make out the shape of a head.

I targeted it, and lowered the axe.

It chopped right through what must have been the neck, then cracked the pavement with a boom. I almost covered my eyes, not wanting to see inside, but my curiosity made me look.

Nothing but wood, just like a tree. That's all she'd been made of. Her entire body ceased moving. I backed away slowly, then felt a hand around my neck.

"Hello, Rachel," said the voice of Mr. Smith.

No.

No way.

I wouldn't be snatched up by one of these salad heads again.

I swung and kicked and even bit his hand, trying to get away.

"That'll give you green teeth, kid," he said, tightening his grip and forcing me to stay still. Then he bent over and picked up a shovel from the ground. "I'll need this. Now let's go. You're going to dig this," he joked, dragging me along with him out of his front yard.

I heard a voice call to us as we left.

"Don't leave me here," begged the separated parts of Mrs. Smith. "The fire will reach me before I can regenerate myself!"

"I can't sacrifice the crop to save you, Betty!" Mr. Smith called back to her. "Something good has to come out of all this trouble!"

"WHERE ARE YOU TAKING ME?!" I demanded as we tracked farther away from the burning house. From that position, I saw the windows blow out and the flames reach for the night air. The house would surely burn to the ground before someone could get to it.

Mr. Smith waited until we had traveled a good distance from the house before he said anything. He stopped and turned my head to face him. The red glow from his burning home struck his face just right for him to look even more sinister. "You've been through so much, I think you should see what this is all about," he said. "It all takes place on the hill you showed Richard and Jane. Let's go take a look, eh?"

We stayed in the shadows of my neighborhood as, one by one, the people on my street came out of their homes to see the Smiths' burning home. Mr. Smith kept a viselike grip on my mouth. I could hardly breathe, much less scream. At about the same time the fire trucks pulled into the entrance of the neighborhood, my captor and I reached the dreaded hill.

I tried to make getting to the top hard for him by making myself dead weight. His strength made this tactic useless, and the higher up we got, the faster he actually went. When we got to the top, he stood me up and wrapped a huge red vine across my mouth and tied it.

"If this rain ever really comes down, they might save a few things in that house, after all. They might even find something incriminating. But by the time they realize anything, it'll be too late. We can take over this town in a week."

"Don't bite down," he said. "It's poisonous."

Then he pulled off one of his own fingers, stretched it to over a foot in length, and bound my wrists with it. The binding tightened on contact, so much so that I felt my fingers begin to swell.

"They also make great bread ties," he joked. "Now come see what I've done to the place!"

He led me to the same spot where Richard Jane, and I had stood just two days before. The land had been completely farmed.

The dirt had been plowed and sectioned into rows. Down every row lay a familiar crop.

Green pumpkins, the same kind I had seen just two months before. They filled every inch of the garden. There must have been at least fifty of them.

"We are very creative with chemicals. Most garden vegetation takes at least a month to grow naturally. But we grow *un*naturally. It takes us just two days. That's how we'll rule in such a short time. You see, what you humans would call a crop, we call 'birth'!" A winning grin crossed his face. "Where do we come from? I could give you many theories to that, but ultimately I don't really know. There's *something*. Something *in the dirt* of Fairfield that spawned us and allows us to *thrive*. I'm so grateful for this very *strange* place.

"Betty, Richard, Jane, and I were the first. After our birth we merged with the land and studied life. We saw how your kind treated the vegetation of the world. *Tearing down trees to build your houses. Growing crops of our own species to harvest and consume.* It was sickening. And we will not let it continue. We formulated a plan to use *your* kind for *our* benefit. We decided to keep our enemies close—to get to know you. Then we could blend in, and you would never know we were dangerous until it was too late. I can't believe it was almost ruined by one curious little girl. But it doesn't matter now. Everything has fallen into place. We . . .

wait!" He held his hand up to shush any noise, keeping his eyes beaded on the garden.

Thumping. I heard thumping.

My eyes scoured the plant shells for the noise, but I didn't see anything.

"It's happening. It's really happening," Mr. Smith muttered.

I used the chance to make one last-ditch effort at an escape. Backing up slowly, I went from toe to heel, peeking carefully behind me so I wouldn't trip over anything. Then a leaf, a small, curled, brown one, blew from the trunk of a tree behind me and landed just under my foot. A crunch followed.

Mr. Smith whipped around, saw me escaping, and got down on his knees. Placing his right hand on the ground, he stared in my direction.

But not at me. *He watched the tree.*

Suddenly, I heard something begin to crack and bend with a sickening whine. I turned and saw it.

The tree had come to life, and it bent over to grab me.

Its limbs curled around my arms and legs and pulled me into the air, where I struggled futilely to get free.

"That's a good spot for you," said Mr. Smith. "You have a good spot for the show."

The thumping got louder and louder . . . then suddenly stopped.

I looked to Mr. Smith for an answer, and by looking over his shoulder, I got one.

The shell of the green pumpkin behind him had cracked, and an oozing slime, just like before, leaked from it like a yolk.

"The next generation of humans won't be human at all," Mr. Smith swore loudly. "They'll be plants! You are witnessing the birth of an army!"

Something poked its way through the crack like a baby bird poking its way out of its shell. This thing couldn't be an animal, yet what came out of that shell looked an awful lot like a hand.

"Glorious!" Mr. Smith raised his voice. "Glorious! They're coming to life! More Plant People!"

25

The rain began to pour down on all of us.

I dangled in the air, horrified at the thought of what might take place in the next few minutes.

What came out of the shells were *shaped* like humans, but consisted of nothing but vegetation. The long, white, spaghetti tentacles I'd seen from the Smith's unfinished roof belonged to the newborn plant creatures. Many of them protruded from the bodies of these infant monsters, making them look like mops. They slowly tore through their shells and crawled out beside them. When they fed their tendrils back into the shells, I guessed that they still received nourishment from them. They all sat beside their birth hulls and nursed.

Mr. Smith stayed out of the garden, pacing slowly along the side. Occasionally, he would stop and take in the sight, and shake his fist in triumph. Then, as the rain continued to come down, he walked to the side of the field to grab something. It looked like a container, something I hadn't noticed before.

There was writing on the side of the container.

I strained to read it, but the rain made that *almost* impossible.

Placing the container on the ground, he reached for a handle jetting from the top of it, and began pumping it in and out. Holding the nozzle, which was attached by a hose, out over the field, he sprayed a bright-green mist over the newborn plants.

"Growing vitamins," Mr. Smith said. I couldn't tell if he was still speaking to me or had taken up talking to himself.

It didn't matter. *I'd had enough.*

A branch hung just an inch from my face. I lifted my head to it, and used it to try to scrape the vine from my mouth. After a couple of tries, I did it.

"AAGGGGGHHHHH! HELP ME! SOME-BODY HELP ME!" I screamed at the top of my lungs, trying to summon the entire neighborhood.

As Mr. Smith turned to me, I started twisting my body in all directions, kicking and screaming like before. I wanted to tear my way out of there.

Mr. Smith held his hand up in the air, making a fist at first, but then opened it.

The tree limbs let me go, and I plummeted to the ground.

"That's it for you, girl," cursed Mr. Smith. "I've let you live long enough. Now my plans can't afford someone like you around. I tried to erase your memories and let you live, but you wouldn't let that happen. So now get ready to meet your end!"

Like a stalking lion, he closed in. He reached to the ground and picked up his shovel.

My legs pulsed with waves of pain from the fall. The landing had freed my hands, but they had taken a good beating from the drop, too. Though it hurt to move, I made them work. Backing along the ground, I barely found the strengh to get to my feet.

"HELP! MR. SMITH IS GOING TO KILL ME!" I shrieked. "They're going to come up here! All of my neighbors, and the firemen and the police! They'll stop you!"

"They can't hear you over the wind, kid," he said coldly, marching toward me and raising the shovel to the air. "They're probably not even outside anymore. Most people hate the rain. I find that funny. My species needs it to live, and your kind make sour faces whenever you get sprinkled on. But as I keep telling myself, you're only human."

Suddenly his whole body began expanding. In the blink of an eye, something wrapped around my foot and tripped me before I could get a running start. Falling, I rolled around to watch Mr. Smith's transformation.

His head grew. The sides extended outward, stretching his face to a sickening width. He quickly lost control of his salivary glands and the soupy drool poured from the sides of his mouth. The teeth dropped from his gums and splashed into the puddles beneath him. Huge new razor-sharp incisors emerged in their places, looking as if they could rip a steel door in two. Under his skin, I saw vines moving about, visibly pulsing like ropy veins. As his head grew, his eyes rolled over the top of his head and his nose flattened out to just two blow holes.

I watched his stomach bloat, increasing to

such a size that the button from his pants shot off and zipped past my head like a bullet. The gut got bigger, and soon his legs collapsed under his enormous girth. He continued to expand, as his trunk became nothing more than a giant veiny bean. His arms disappeared into his sides, sucked inside his increasing mass. Only his fingers remained visible, then they, too, came to life. Like Crazy String, they shot into the air, then hit the wet ground like a net full of eels. They separated, each one moving as if it had a mind of its own. Then, simultaneously, they all turned to me.

"Hello, Rachel," said Mr. Smith-monster, now a green, slobbering football-shaped head holding itself just inches from my face.

Two of his slithering fingers picked up the shovel. The Smith-monster lurched back, holding the instrument above his head, about to swat me like a fly.

"Goodbye, Rachel," he forewarned.

My nerves froze. Every muscle tensed. My mind could find nothing to fill it as I realized this image, a twisted creature of another kind, would be the last thing I'd ever see.

Then there was a flash of light.

The shovel fell.

I closed my eyes at that instant, practically blinded. But the vision of what I had seen was burned into my mind.

26

I opened my eyes slowly as I felt a familiar wave of heat brush against my face.

Mr. Smith, King of the Plant People, was on fire.

The smoking shovel beside me left more proof. When he held that steel instrument in the air, it made him a target as well.

Lightning had struck him.

It set him on fire instantly, and now the monster who had seemed so in control just seconds before howled in pain.

As the rain fell harder, I knew the flames would die soon. I had to act fast.

Grabbing the shovel, I thrust it right into the monster's belly and started to push. It took everything I had to move it, and I groaned out loud at the strain it put on me. The fiery tentacles swiped at me, but I dodged them, forging ahead until I felt the shovel sink farther into its gut. I pulled it out and stepped back.

As the burning plant-head of Mr. Smith reached down to snatch me with its teeth, I swung the shovel.

Direct hit.

I smashed the metal into his head so hard he fell back, and his teeth went flying through the air. I moved in again while he lay squirming. Once again, I jammed the shovel into the burning mass and pushed. The rain had made the ground slick, perfect for me to slide the monster to exactly where it would do the most damage.

The crop.

You see, I was finally able to read what it said on that container. I counted on that word with my very life. As I forced the monster forward, it kept running through my head again and again.

FLAMMABLE, FLAMMABLE, FLAMMA-BLE . . .

My eyes focused on the larva-stage Plant People, who had emerged from their shells, but were still too insecure to wander far away from them. They watched wide-eyed as I barreled through the mud with their burning leader. The flames from the terrible, squalling mass tried to kiss my face, but I dodged each of them. I dug in and heaved my hideously unnatural neighbor the last few inches into his garden of monsters.

Some of the flames jumped, sparking little areas. The newborn Plant People instinctively reacted, vining out and attempting to creep away. I knew I'd have to help the fire spread, and quickly.

I picked up the nozzle, and aimed it straight at Mr. Smith's burning head.

In agony, the monster turned toward me.

"You can't kill us," he growled. "It may sound funny, but our roots run deep! We'll be everywhere! We'll know everything! We'll be right there beside you, and you won't know it until it's too late! Make no mistake, the world will be ours!"

"Wow, and you're sure you're not the least bit human?" I asked, as the hatchlings scurried in all directions, spreading over the entire field.

"I'm certain," Mr. Smith snarled, spitting out the words. "Why?"

"Just curious," I answered, then squeezed the trigger with a clear conscience.

Mr. Smith screamed in agony as the mist

blew over him, fueling the flames. The fire blew outward as if thrown by a torch, and attacked the escaping monsters. Each of them ignited, filling the air with terrible shrieks of pain. In blazing motion, the whole field of plants dropped to the ground, burning.

I stayed out there in the rain and watched them burn for thirty minutes. Then, even after their flames finally died, I looked on for another two hours, just to make sure they were dead.

After that, I went home.

27

"And you expect me to believe all of this?" asked Tessa over the phone.

"Believe or don't believe it. It's the truth. But if you think it's just a story, you wouldn't be any different than anyone else," I told her as I stood to look out my window at the blackened remains of the Smith home. Thankfully, the rain had put Richard and Jane out before they could cause any serious damage to my house. But my dad still wonders where the massive charred spot on the back patio came from.

"Well, if it is true, your parents would have to believe you. It happened to them, too," she said.

"Nope. They don't remember a thing. It's like that whole day is just a blank in their lives. All they remember is waking up in bed the next morning with horrendous headaches. Dad said the Smiths sure could throw a party."

"Well, didn't anyone find any remains of those Plant People?" she asked, clearly becoming more of a believer by the second.

"They just dissolved away. I saw some of them disappear on the hill that night. Believe me, I've thought of everything. There's no proof that these things ever existed," I said as someone knocked on my door.

I opened it and found Mom in the doorway, smiling and holding my lunch under a plate cover.

"Mmmmm . . . PastaRoni," I said. "Just the way I like it—straight from the can." I grabbed the covered plate and placed it on my bed.

Mom closed the door with a smile, leaving me to my conversation.

"You're not on your diet anymore?" Tessa asked. "I thought you had to stay in shape for cheerleading."

"Not anymore. I quit," I answered, ignoring my lunch for awhile and sitting back down on the floor to talk.

"YOU QUIT? WHY?" she asked in disbelief.

"Because I never liked it, really," I said. "And I was only doing it to get people to notice me.   Lately, I really haven't cared that much about being popular. If it happens, cool. If it doesn't, so what? I'm all wrapped up in my new interests lately, anyway."

"What's that?" Tessa wanted to know.

"Fires," I answered. "Ever since this mess happened, I've been really interested in them. I'm considering the fire department someday. I figure that since I started so many, it's only right that I stop a few, too."

Tessa laughed, then grew quiet.

"You know, Rachel, if it's really true, how can you trust your parents?" she asked.

"What do you mean, Tessa?"

"Well, they were held prisoner in that basement while those plants did who-knows-what to their brains. How do you know it didn't turn them into slaves, agents of the Plant People?" she asked.

"Because they're my parents! I'd notice any unusual behavior," I told her.

"Okay, what about that plant that attacked you in the locker room? It got away, right? What if that plant came after you?" Tessa persisted.

"I hadn't thought of that," I admitted.

"If your parents are plant-zombies, they could let the plant right in your house and you wouldn't even know. You could be in your room, talking on the phone, and the plant could bust right in on you. Or better yet, your plant-zombie-mother could sneak it in there . . ."

I knew Tessa just wanted to freak me out. She liked making me paranoid. But knowing that didn't keep me from staring at the covered plate Mom brought up.

I suddenly realized that the plate wasn't warm. Also, since when did Mom serve things under a cover anyway? I was dying to know what was under it, so I got closer to have a look.

"Yep, there could be plants out there waiting for you to come out of the house at any time. They probably all want revenge," Tessa kept babbling.

I knelt right beside it, and grabbed hold of the handle.

"Everywhere you turn, they'll be there," Tessa said.

My stomach started doing somersaults. Beads of sweat formed on my forehead. The dryness of my lips made them crack. And no matter how hard I tried, I couldn't swallow the lump in my throat.

My heart stopped the second I lifted the cover.

"Oh, no. *NO!*" I screamed.

On the plate lay the last thing I ever wanted to see.

Celery.

About the Authors

Marty M. Engle and **Johnny Ray Barnes Jr.**, graduates of the Art Institute of Atlanta, are the creators, writers, designers, and illustrators of the **Strange Matter**™ series and the **Strange Matter**™ World Wide Web page.

Their interests and expertise range from state-of-the-art 3-D computer graphics and interactive multimedia, to books and scripts (television and motion picture).

Marty lives in La Jolla, California, with his wife Jana and twin terror pets, Polly and Oreo.

Johnny Ray lives in Tierrasanta, California, and spends every free moment with his fiancée, Meredith.

And now
an exciting preview
of the next

#15 Creature Features

by Marty M. Engle

I almost fell asleep *despite* the screaming.

After awhile, the loud piercing shrieks just drummed inside my head, more an annoyance than anything else.

Would she please just shut up?!

A victim's scream comes in many different flavors. Some are pure vanilla, like a shallow, half-hearted wheeze. Some are musical, a perfect sustained note, unwavering in pitch or volume. Some are inverted gasps of surprise *pretending* to be screams, like nasally air being sucked in instead of blown out.

Sometimes you get lucky.

Sometimes you hear a deep, rich and satisfying scream. Kind of a throaty, wet scream that comes deep from inside the gut. The kind of scream that makes you feel the horror as if it were your very own. The kind that's liberating. The kind that sets your brain on fire and brings an unintentional smile to your face.

Not so this time. My name is Jonathan Drake. So far, my friends and I have suffered through every type of scream except the last.

"OW!" I cried, surprised at the elbow in my ribs. "Cut it out!"

"Wake up, Jon! You're missing the best part!" Nate hissed, dribbling bits of wet popcorn from the corners of his mouth.

I felt my blood begin to boil. "There *is* no best part. You know why there is no best part? Because I've seen this movie before. I saw it when it was *Bloodinator*. I saw it when it was *B2: Blood Wars* and I saw it when it was *Bloodinator's Revenge!* And you know what, Nate? IT WAS BETTER THE FIRST THREE TIMES!"

A barrage of shushes reigned down on my head.

Thanks to my good friend, Nathan, I emerged from my semi-conscious state and back into the flickering nightmare that was *Bloodinator IV: Renegade.*

My tired eyes were reluctantly drawn to the flickering screen and to the ridiculous antics of the blood-crazed cyborg. I pulled my hand down across my face, trying to get a little feeling back.

I moaned. "Oh, look at this. Now he'll have a last-minute, heart-warming heart-to-heart with his soon-to-be wounded commando friend who will most certainly die in about fifteen minutes."

A type-three scream from the screen.

"Or less."

I shifted in my seat. "After this, he'll find out his one-time partner is really his enemy, then his girl will turn out to be working for the other side."

"Jon, please," Nate slurped.

"Then he'll wind up hanging off either (a) a cliff (b) a tall building or (c) a catwalk in a warehouse that probably doesn't serve any structural purpose, other than to have him *hang* off it."

"Are you trying to ruin it for us, John?"

"The head villain, instead of getting away while he can, will wind up towering over Bloodinator and he'll either hold a gun to his head or step on his fingers, or both."

"Point made, Jon," Nate munched.

"At which time, he'll say some stupid one

liner, grab the villain (incredibly moronic for being there in the first place), and throw him screaming over the side to his death."

"You finished?" Nate asked.

"Time check," I grumbled.

"7:45," Nate snapped.

"WHAT?! You gotta be kidding me."

Nathan slurped his Coke.

"No." I groaned, leaning forward and rested my head against the seat in front of me. Ah, a dirty wad of gum on the floor. At least there was something interesting to look at.

For three hours.

Bloodinator movies were notoriously long, and lucky me . . . this was a director's cut.

"That was absolutely the worst of the series!" I moaned, bursting through the twin doors and marching out with the rest of the weak-kneed crowd. My friends Nathan, Albert, and Simon, strode beside me through the lobby, seven dollars lighter but with heavy hearts.

"I told you! I knew it! The ending came out of nowhere! You could tell that they put it in at the last second. Kantanka should have gotten away scott free. There was no possible reason for him to come back and fight Bloodinator like that. NONE! That happened strictly so he could get his butt kicked by the hero."

"You're right. Of the series, this had the least amount of story and, by far, the worst tacked-on ending," Albert agreed.

Albert was always quick to agree. Of the gang, he was the only other *serious* critic. Of course, he usually agreed with me. I could never tell if it was because he truly felt that way, or if he just wanted to be my friend. Albert had few friends, and one too many star-geek posters on his wall. Still, he actually did have half-a-clue when it came to movies. Sometimes he could really surprise you with a keen, insightful remark.

"The effects were cool, though," Simon insisted.

Simon White. Illustrator, cartoonist, smart-mouth extraordinaire. He always liked the visuals, especially computer visuals, but could care less about content and character. He *always* paid more attention to the look instead of the story. We had a lot of similar arguments about comic books. Who was more important, the artist or the writer?

I countered, "Yeah, the effects were good, but it's like Chinese food, a half-hour later you forget you even ate!"

"Just a minute, guys," Nate said, vanishing into the boys' room.

Nate didn't care about all this stuff. To him it was just a movie, nothing more. Certainly nothing to argue about. To Nate, it was just a way for the four of us to be together and do something.

I couldn't think that way. Movies were too important to me. I cared about everything in them and I noticed things about them the others didn't. From the name of the cinematographer to the type of film processing they used.

Nate popped back out smiling, "Where to now, guys?"

As if he had to ask. He already knew. It was a Friday night tradition after a lousy horror or action flick.

We had a special place to hang out and talk about it. There, we'd flush out the horrible aftertaste of *The Bloodinator* with remembrances of good movies from the past.

Out on the edge of town, there's an old

abandoned drive-in that's been closed for years. Since the fifties, I think.

The Starlight Drive-In. The tall neon sign still towers over the road, all broken and overgrown with vines.

So is the screen. There are big holes that flap when the wind whips through them.

The old speaker posts, yellow metal flaked with rest, line the parking field like grave markers. Some still have the speakers.

The projection booth is in the top of the concession stand. That's the creepiest place. It still has the projector. We've even tried to get it to run a few times, but of course it wouldn't.

I heard they tried to tear it down once but couldn't.

According to the story, only one of the demolition guys survived. When they found him hiding in the concession stand he was curled in a ball and shaking, moaning to himself. His hair had turned snow white and he had completely lost his mind.

They never found the others and the story the one survivor told was just too unbelievable to be true.

Or so I thought.

CONTINUE THE
ADVENTURE...

**with the StrangeMatter™ library.
Experience a terrifying new
StrangeMatter™ adventure every month.**